W IS FOR WAPITI!
AN ALPHABET SONGBOOK

SONGS BY CHRISTIANE DUCHESNE AND PAUL KUNIGIS
PERFORMED BY KAREN YOUNG AND GLEN BOWSER
ILLUSTRATED BY GENEVIÈVE CÔTÉ

Aha! Aha! Did you do that?

Aha! Aha! Did you do that?
No, it wasn't me, oh no, it wasn't me
Aha! Aha! Was it you who did that?
No, it wasn't me, oh no, it wasn't me

Who put a tiny mouse on the cat's bed in the house?
Who hid the toy car in the oatmeal cookie jar?
It wasn't me, no, no, it wasn't me

Who plopped a slimy toad on my pie à la mode?
Who stuffed a bath mat inside my favorite hat?
It wasn't me, no, no, it wasn't me

So... who... did?
I'll never tell!

Itsy-Bitsy Tiny Boat

B

A tiny little boat for you
Itsy-bitsy tiny boat
A tiny little boat
So paper thin
It rocks you
It cradles you
It carries you off
It whisks you away

A tiny little boat for you
Itsy-bitsy tiny boat
A tiny little boat
So paper thin
And you're off
Off and away
Far far away
Every day

Everyday you sail away
On a paper thin boat

Sail back to me

Clickety Cluck the Duck

I love playing in my tub
Rub-a-dub-dub
With all my fishy friends
And my duck
Clickety Cluck

There's a hungry goldfish
Who eats the soap in the dish
But not my duck
Clickety Cluck

There's a fish who's all alone
He doesn't have a home
Neither does my duck
Clickety Cluck

The green fish, he's a clown
He swims upside down
And the blue fish
He's got his tail in a knot

At night, the fish who's black
Sings "Yakkity yak"
And he wakes up
Clickety Cluck

But the yellow fish
But... but what's he up to?
He's tickling me

I love playing in my tub
Rub-a-dub-dub
With all my fishy friends
And my duck
Clickety-Cluck

D Love to Dream

Love to dream
Love to dream
Love to dream
Dream, dream, dream

Sweet dreams to you
You and you and to me too

I just love to dream

Mister Elephant

Good day, Mister Elephant, good day
You've come by to say, good day
You want to come in?
No, you're much too wide
My home is too small
Will you please wait outside?
Are you thirsty?
Of course, I'll get you some water
No, no, don't come in
It's really no bother, wait right where you are
Here's the glass, here you go
Just slip your long trunk through the window
My home is too small, you will not fit at all
You can't fit in my home
Besides you're full-grown
But my home, my home...
Who will fix my home sweet home?

All of the children, the children, the children
All of the elephant's children
They will repair, will repair, will repair what is broken

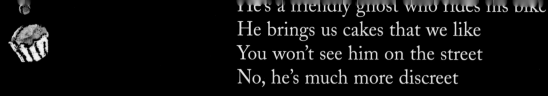

He's a friendly ghost who rides his bike
He brings us cakes that we like
You won't see him on the street
No, he's much more discreet

F The Fruit-Filled Flans of the Friendly Ghost

We like the cakes, we like the pies
But the sweets we love the most
Are the fruit-filled flans
Of the friendly ghost

I'm a Twisted Turtle
With a Goofy Grin

G

Inside my carapace
I wear a funny face
But no one can tell
What's underneath
My shell

I'm a twisted turtle
With a goofy grin
I'm a twisted turtle
With a goofy grin

Inside my carapace
I wear a funny face
If you don't want to see
You mustn't look at me

I'm a twisted turtle
With a goofy grin
I'm a twisted turtle
With a goofy grin
I'm a twisted turtle
With a hairy chin
I'm a proud
And glorious chelonian

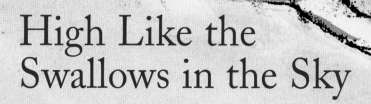

High Like the Swallows in the Sky

H

One day I'll fly high
Like the swallows in the sky
One day you'll see me
Perched upon a poplar tree

One day I'll fly high
Like the swallows in the sky
One day you'll see me
Perched upon a cherry tree

I saw them gliding
Now they're hiding
Where did the swallows go?

One day I'll fly high
Like the swallows in the sky
One day you'll see me
Perched upon an apple tree

One day I'll fly high
Like the swallows in the sky
One day you'll see me
Perched upon…

I saw them gliding
Now they're hiding
Where did the swallows go?

One day I'll follow
The white-chested swallow
I'll know
Where the swallows go

Imagine That

I

Imagine that

They come from books that I've read
They float into my head
Pictures go by
Like clouds in the sky

When I close my eyes
I see them as I like
Pictures go by
Like clouds in the sky

John the Pigeon

J

John the pigeon
John the pigeon has four legs, four legs
One, two, three, four
One, two, three, four

John the pigeon has four legs
That's twice as many feet
To tap to the beat
Than a pigeon who has two legs
It's the coolest strut on the street

John the pigeon has four legs?
Imagine that!
Yeah… what's wrong with four legs?
But a pigeon only has two legs…
Oh, not John the pigeon !

K

Mister Ka the Koala

Mister Ka the Koala
Has four kids
Armani, Tapio, Mo and Pol

Armani Ka, Tapio Ka
And Mo Ka

And Pol...
He hates being called Pol Ka

Little Louisa Damselfly

Little Louisa Damselfly
You blow bubbles
Tell me why

My bubble is my home
When I'm inside it it, I can roam

Little Louisa Damselfly
How many bubbles may I buy?

I'll give one to you
Now what will you do?

Little Louisa Damselfly
In my bubble, I will fly

M My Marmot and Me

Every morning
I spend time with my bunny
Grab some carrots
The day is so sunny
Every morning
On the way to the garden
A marmot pops up
And says to me,
"Good day!
Have you come to play?"

I say, "No, can't you see?
It's time for my bunny and me"

'Round about noon
I spend time with my mouse
I pack up some cookies
Then I leave the house
'Round about noon
Beneath my umbrella
A marmot pops up
And says to me,
"Good day!
Do you want to play?"

I say; "No, can't you see?
It's time for my black wolf and me"

My poor, poor marmot, I know it's not fair
No carrots, no cookies, no stories to share
But tomorrow here's what we'll do
I'll come by with something especially for you

Hey, Groundhog
What would you like from me?

"All that I want is this:
Just give me a sweet little kiss"

I say, "No, can't you see?
It's time for my mouse and me"

Late in the evening, my black wolf and I
We read 'The old lady who swallowed a fly'
Late in the evening, on the side of the path
A marmot pops up and says to me,
"Gee! Will you read to me?"

When My Nose is Numb

N

When my nose is numb
It's time to go inside

In wintertime
I swim, I jump, I fly
In wintertime
I swim in snowflakes

In wintertime
I swim, I jump, I fly
In wintertime
I jump in the snowbanks

In wintertime
I swim, I jump, I fly
In wintertime
I fly like the wind in the sky

One Plus Two
Plus Three Oval Eggs

O

Mrs. Grass Snake laid an egg
Mrs. Turtle laid two eggs
Mrs. Chicken laid three eggs
One plus two plus three
Makes six

Six oval eggs
That will hatch
Let's get ready to catch… what
One baby snake
Two baby turtles
And three little chicks

Mrs. Duck, she laid an egg
Mrs. Crow laid two eggs
Mrs. Ostrich laid three eggs
One plus two plus three makes six

Six oval eggs
That will hatch
Let's get ready to catch…what?
One little duckling
Two baby crows
And three ostrich chicks

One little duck
Two baby crows
And three ostrich chicks

PQR

Papa's Quiet Rascals

Daddy, oh Daddy
Will you sing me a song?
I'd like to hear the one
About the four kitty cats

Papa's quiet rascals
Lying under the bed
No one can see them there
It's dark under the bed

Papa's quiet rascals
Are really quite rambunctious
Purring, snoring, hissing, growling
Papa's quiet rascals

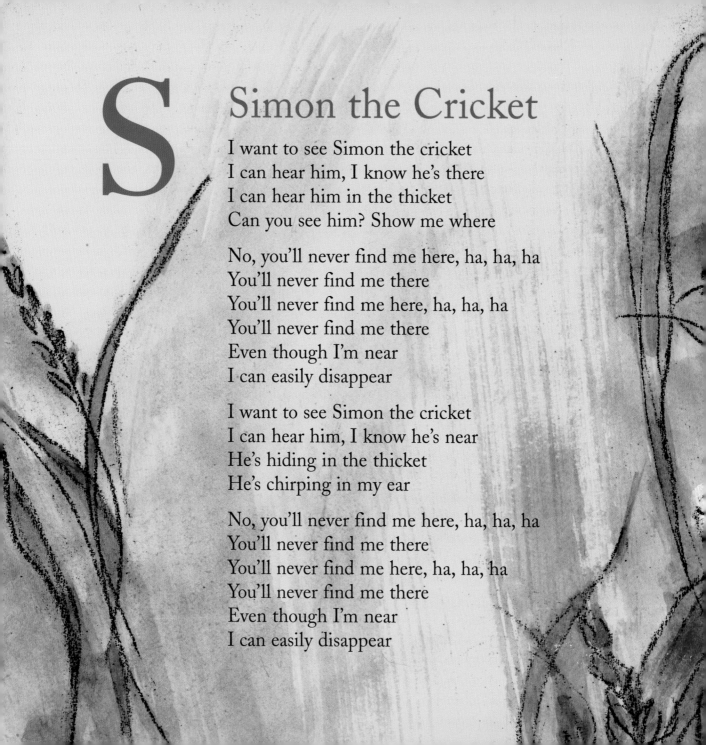

S Simon the Cricket

I want to see Simon the cricket
I can hear him, I know he's there
I can hear him in the thicket
Can you see him? Show me where

No, you'll never find me here, ha, ha, ha
You'll never find me there
You'll never find me here, ha, ha, ha
You'll never find me there
Even though I'm near
I can easily disappear

I want to see Simon the cricket
I can hear him, I know he's near
He's hiding in the thicket
He's chirping in my ear

No, you'll never find me here, ha, ha, ha
You'll never find me there
You'll never find me here, ha, ha, ha
You'll never find me there
Even though I'm near
I can easily disappear

Too Much

T

Too, too much
I love you too much

Too, too much
I love you so very much

Too, too, too much
I love you way too much

I love you even more
Than horses running free
Than castles by the sea
Than…

What is bigger than love so true?
I love you and you love me too

Just One Unit?

One
Just one?
Now there are two
Now there are three
Three what?
Three units!

U-N-I-T-S

Let's count to ten

One, two, three, four, five
Six, seven, eight, nine, ten

Oops!
We forgot the zero!

V VIPs of the Earth

We are the kings of the earth
Believe us when we say
Without us there would be no berrie
No tomatoes, corn or hay

Nothing to eat for the herds of sheep
For the cows and for the dogs
Without us, without us
Nothing in the ground
Would ever grow
Oh no, no, no, no, no

We till the soil, we give it air
It's work that no one sees
We are the worms and we have flair
We are the earth's VIPs

They're so ugly and slimy!
We are the kings of the earth
It wouldn't be too nice
If there were no more carrots
No cabbage and no rice

Nothing of course for
the camel, the horse
The lions or the hogs
Without us, without us
Nothing in the ground
Would ever grow
Oh no, no, no, no, no

Do you think I'm lying?
If we didn't spend our days
Tilling the soil
It would be as hard
As rock, rock, rock, rock 'n' roll!

We till the soil, we give it air
It's work that no one sees
You'd be doomed
Without our derrières
We are the earth's VIPs

We are the worms
We are the earth's VIPs

W

A Humongous Wapiti

Deep in the forest
Amongst the trees
There lives a humongous Wapiti
Who, when young, legends say
Could scare the hunters away

X

The Xylophone and the Yoyo

X is for xylophone
X is always for xylophone

If you have a yoyo that's yellow and blue
Spin the two colours into something new

If you spin a yoyo that's yellow and blue
You'll have a nice green yoyo

Y

Zoom, Zoom, Zoom

Z

Zoom, zoom, zoom
Our song's at an end
And the storybook is over
Zoom, zoom, zoom
Our song's at an end
Shall we zoom zoom once again?

If our song's at an end
And the storybook is over
Shall we zoom zoom once again?

Let's do it again

Let's Sing It Again

A, B, C, D, E, F, G, H, I, J, K, L, M, N, O, P, Q, R, S, T, U, V, W, X, Y, Z.

 A   is for "Aha! Aha! Did you do that?"

 B   is for a boat made of paper on which you sail away

 C   is for Clickety Cluck, my rubber duck

 D   is for "I love to dream, dream, dream"

 E   is for the elephant who came into my house

 F   is for the fruit-filled flans of the friendly ghost

 G   is for the goofy grin that the turtle wears

 H   is for up high with the swallows in the sky

 I   is for "Imagine that." You can imagine anything in your head

 J   is for John the pigeon who taps his four legs to the beat

 K   is for Mister Ka, the koala, and his four kids

 L   is for Little Louisa Damselfly

 M   is for my marmot and me, and for my mommy too!

 N   is for my nose that gets numb

O is for one, plus two, plus three oval eggs

 P is for Papa

 Q is for quiet kitty cats sleeping under the bed

 R is for the rambunctious rascals making a racket

 S is for Simon the cricket

 T is for too much, I love you way too much

 U is for units. Count them: one, two, three.

 V is for VIP, you know, the worms

 W is for the humungous wapiti who lives in the forest

 X is for xylophone. The X is always for xylophone!
Why is it that the X is always for xylophone?

 Y is for my yoyo that's yellow and blue

 Z is for zoom through it again because our song's already through

And now you know your ABC's!

Singers Karen Young and Glen Bowser Lyrics Christiane Duchesne and Paul Kunigis Music Paul Kunigis
Record Producer Paul Kunigis Artistic Director Roland Stringer Design Stephan Lorti for Haus Design
Translation Consultant Michelle Campagne Copy Editor Ruth Joseph Recorded and mixed by François Lalonde at
Studio Chez Frank Piano recorded by Alexandre Pampalon à Surf Studio Children's voices recorded by Davy Gallan
at Dogger Pond Music Mastering by Guy Hébert at Studio Karisma

Children's voices Luka Gallant *Little Louisa Damselfly, Aha! Aha! Did You Do That?, Mister Elephant, My Nose is Nur*
Just One Unit?, Let's Sing It Again Mia Gallant *High Like the Swallows in the Sky, Aha! Aha! Did You Do That?, Miste*
Elephant, My Nose is Numb, Just One Unit?, Let's Sing It Again Toby Gallant *Papa's Quiet Rascals, Aha! Aha! Did You D*
That?, Mister Elephant, My Nose is Numb, Just One Unit?, Let's Sing It Again

Musicians Paul Kunigis piano, wurlitzer Bruno Rouyère acoustic and electric guitar André Dédé Vander bass
José Major drums François Lalonde drums, percussions, xylophone, glockenspiel, vibraphone
Caroline Meunier accordion Jean-Denis Levasseur clarinet, piccolo, recorder, saxophone Claude St-Jean trombone
Jean Savbourin souzaphone, bass trumpet Kristine Molnar violin Didier Dumoutier accordion (*Clickety Cluck the Du*
My Marmot and Me, One Plus Two Plus Three Oval Eggs) Yves Desrosiers banjo, acoustic guitar
(*Mister Ka the Koala*), electric guitar (*VIPs Of The Earth*), pedal steel guitar (*Mister Elephant*)

Ⓡ www.thesecretmountain.com

Ⓒ Ⓟ 2012 The Secret Mountain (Folle Avoine Productions)

ISBN-10 2-923163-83-4 / ISBN-13 978-2-923163-83-3